# BRADFORD STREET BUDDIES
# Springtime Blossoms

For Chloe Bell, another little blossom.  —J.N.
To educators everywhere, thank you for all you do!  —M.H.

Text copyright © 2017 by Jerdine Nolen
Illustrations copyright © 2017 by Michelle Henninger
First Green Light Readers edition 2017

For information about permission to reproduce selections from this book,
write to trade.permissions@hmhco.com or to Permissions, Houghton Mifflin
Harcourt Publishing Company, 3 Park Avenue, 19th Floor, New York, New York 10016.

www.hmhco.com

The text of this book is set in Chaparral Pro.
The display type was set in Candy Round and Marujo.
The illustrations are drawn in ink and watercolor on Arches watercolor paper.

Library of Congress Cataloging-in-Publication Data
Names: Nolen, Jerdine, author. | Henninger, Michelle, illustrator.
Title: Springtime blossoms / written by Jerdine Nolen ; illustrated by
Michelle Henninger.
Description: Boston ; New York : Houghton Mifflin Harcourt, 2017. | Series:
Bradford Street buddies ; book 3 | Series: Green Light Readers. Level 3 |
Summary: It's springtime on Bradford Street and twins Jada and Jamal
Perkins are helping their parents with yardwork as they look for signs of
spring. When their teacher tells them about the town's plans to plant new
trees at school in celebration of Earth Day, Jada and Jamal and their best
friends, Carlita and Josh, come up with a school beautification project of
their own."—Provided by publisher.
Identifiers: LCCN 2016008848| ISBN 9780544873902 (trade paper) | ISBN
9780544873919 (paper over board)
Subjects: | CYAC: Spring—Fiction. | Flowers—Fiction. | Community
life—Fiction. | Earth Day—Fiction. | African Americans—Fiction.
Classification: LCC PZ7.N723 Sp 2017 | DDC [E]—dc23
LC record available at https://lccn.loc.gov/2016008848

Manufactured in China
SCP 10 9 8 7 6 5 4 3 2 1
4500634145

# BRADFORD STREET BUDDIES
# Springtime Blossoms

WRITTEN BY JERDINE NOLEN

ILLUSTRATED BY MICHELLE HENNINGER

**Green Light Readers**
HOUGHTON MIFFLIN HARCOURT
Boston  New York

# CONTENTS

# 1. Signs of Spring

It was homework time in the Perkins house. Jada and Jamal were thinking very hard, but they really wanted to go outside and play.

Jada heard something.
*CHIRP! CHIRP! CHIRP!*

She ran to the window. Jamal followed along.
So did Snuggly and Cuddly.
"A robin! My first sign of spring!" announced Jada.
"Now I need only two more things for my list."

"I found something for *my* list," chuckled Jamal.

"What?" Jada asked.

"Mom and Dad working in the yard!" said Jamal.

"And Muzzy is helping."

"That is a sure sign of spring," giggled Jada.

3

It was a sunny afternoon on Bradford Street.

Mr. Perkins was trimming trees and bushes.

Mrs. Perkins was planting flowers.

"Can we come outside now?" asked Jamal.

Muzzy barked. He wanted them to come outside too.

"Is your homework done?" Mrs. Perkins asked.

"We're doing it now," said Jada.

"We can finish it quicker outside," added Jamal.

"Mrs. Pritchett wants us to find signs of spring,"
Jada explained.

"Can we come outside, please?" begged Jamal.

"Sure," laughed Mr. Perkins.

"It's too nice to be inside anyway."

"I see birds building a nest,"
Jamal shouted.

"I found a fuzzy caterpillar!"
exclaimed Jada.

6

"Yes, spring is blossoming all around us," said
Mrs. Perkins. "The purple crocuses are already
poking through the ground."

Jada and Jamal collected the big pile of branches
Mr. Perkins had cut.
"What should we do with these sticks?" asked Jada.

"They're not *just* sticks," explained Mr. Perkins.
"They're forsythia and cherry tree branches."
"Oh," said Jamal.
"We'll keep some and give some to Mrs. Garcia,"
said Mrs. Perkins.

"Why would *anyone* want a bunch of dried-up branches?" asked Jada.

"Look closely," answered Mrs. Perkins. "They aren't dried up at all."

"Oooh! I see tiny yellow buds," observed Jada.

"I see pink buds on these," said Jamal.

"Mrs. Garcia wants to use some of the branch cuttings to grow new bushes and trees in her yard," said Mr. Perkins. "She can bring some inside, too. They'll brighten up the house."

"That's right," agreed Mrs. Perkins. "The buds will blossom in a vase filled with water in a warm house." Jada looked at Jamal and shrugged.
"I didn't know that!" she said.

"Maybe Josh and Mr. Cornell would like some branches too," said Jamal. "I'll go ask."
"I'll go with you," said Jada. "My list is all done now."
"Mine too!" said Jamal.

## 2. A Colorful Surprise

The next morning there was a colorful surprise in
the kitchen. Mr. and Mrs. Perkins were right.
The buds had opened into yellow and pink blossoms.

"Now *our* house is blooming all over," laughed Jamal.
"Could we bring a bouquet of branches to school for
Mrs. Pritchett?" Jada asked.
Mrs. Perkins smiled.
"I made two extra bouquets last night," she said.
Jada and Jamal clapped.

On the way to school, the twins saw Carlita and Josh.
"We're bringing some branches to school for
Mrs. Pritchett," announced Jamal.

"Did your branches bloom?" asked Jada.
"Oh, yes," Carlita said. "The blossoms gave my mom
the best idea. She made pink blossom cupcakes for our
deli."

"Mmm," said Josh. "Spring *is* blossoming and yummy."

When the four friends arrived at school, they saw a truck delivering trees.

Mrs. Pritchett waved to her students.

"Look at all the trees being unloaded from the truck," Jamal said.

"Where did they come from?" Josh asked.
"And where are they going?" wondered Carlita.

"Come inside, boys and girls," said Mrs. Pritchett. "I
will tell you all about it!"

"Today is Earth Day," began Mrs. Pritchett. "It's a special day to celebrate spring and the beauty of our Earth. Planting trees and flowers helps our Earth."

"As I like to say," she continued, "people and plants make perfect partners."
Jada raised her hand. "But what about all the new trees?" she asked.

"Our city donated the trees in celebration of Earth Day," explained Mrs. Pritchett. "The workers are planting them now. When they're done, we'll take a walk to see them and find signs of spring."
The class cheered.

## 3. Plans Blossom

Mrs. Pritchett's class walked all around the school. There were new trees planted in front of the school and at the back of the playground.

"Look at our new trees," Mrs. Pritchett said. "Spring makes everything look beautiful and new."

When they were back inside, Mrs. Pritchett asked,
"What signs of spring did you see?"

"The trees were nice," said Jamal.
"The grass is getting a little greener," said Josh.

"But there are no flowers blooming," said Jada. "Besides the new trees, spring is not blossoming at our school," decided Carlita.

"Perhaps spring needs a little help," suggested Mrs. Pritchett. "Remember, people and plants make perfect partners."

"Maybe we could plant an Earth Day flower garden," said Jada.

"We could put flowers between the new trees near the wall," added Josh.

"It would be so pretty," said Carlita.

"Maybe our parents would help," said Jamal.

"That's a wonderful idea!" Mrs. Pritchett said. "I'll check to see if we can plant a garden on Saturday!"
The children clapped and cheered.

During the week, there was a lot of excitement in
Mrs. Pritchett's class. The children planned the garden.
Parents brought in flowers and planting supplies.
Mrs. Perkins brought daffodil bulbs.
Mrs. Garcia brought daisies.

Once Mrs. Pritchett talked with some of the parents, she had more exciting news. "After we plant the garden, we will have a picnic!" she said.

Now Mrs. Pritchett's class was blooming all over.

# 4. Picture Perfect

On Saturday, the playground was busy. Mr. Perkins and Mr. Cornell used shovels to turn over the soil. Other parents used hoes to make rows.

Some children painted rocks to border the garden. Other children helped Mrs. Pritchett pull weeds. Mrs. Garcia and Mrs. Perkins organized the picnic.

Everyone helped to plant the flowers.
The children dug holes and pushed the roots of the
plants into the soil.
Then they covered them over.

In no time Mrs. Pritchett's class had planted their
Earth Day garden.
The trees were new. The flowers were beautiful.
"Spring makes everything look new again,"
sighed Mrs. Pritchett.

"But that gray wall behind the garden does not look so beautiful and new," Carlita said.

"It looks ugly," said Jada.

"We should do something about it!" Josh said.

"Like what?" said Jamal.

The kids formed a huddle.

"What could make the wall look better?" asked Carlita.

"My dad always says a little paint
can make *anything* look new again," said Josh.

"That's a great idea!" Jamal said.

"We could paint flowers on the wall!" exclaimed
Carlita.

"We could paint our school on it too," said Josh.

"The picture would remind us of all the fun we had
planting our garden," Jada squealed.

"I know where we can get a ladder and more paint," said Josh.

"I'll get the brushes we used to paint the rocks," said Carlita.

"I'll see if there are more brushes in our classroom!" added Jada.

"I have an idea for a special message on the wall," said Jamal.

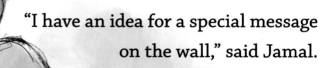

And together, Mrs. Pritchett's class planted *and* painted a very colorful garden!

People and Plants
Make Perfect
Partners